B J. H.

The Child's Bijou

B J. H.

The Child's Bijou

ISBN/EAN: 9783337218027

Printed in Europe, USA, Canada, Australia, Japan

Cover: Foto ©Andreas Hilbeck / pixelio.de

More available books at **www.hansebooks.com**

THE CHILD'S

BIJOU

Edited by J. H. B.

BUFFALO:
BREED, BUTLER & CO.
1861.

CONTENTS.

THE GREEN PASTURES.

I walked in a field of fresh clo-
  ver this morn,
  Where lambs played so mer-
    rily under the trees,
Or rubbed their soft coats on a
  naked old thorn,
  Or nibbled the clover, or
    rested at ease.

And under the hedge ran a
  clear water-brook,
  To drink from when thirsty,
    or weary with pain;
And so gay did the daisies and
  buttercups look,
  That I thought little lambs
    must be happy all day.

And when I remember the
  beautiful psalm,
    That tells about Christ and
    his pastures so green,
I know He is willing to make me
  His lamb,
    And happier far than the
    lambs I have seen.

If I drink of the waters so peace-
  ful and still,
    That flow in His field, I forev-
    er shall live;
If I love Him, and seek His
  commands to fulfil,
    A place in his sheepfold to me
    He will give.

The lambs are at peace in the
  fields when they play;

The long summer's day in con-
tentment they spend ;
But happier I, if in God's holy
way
I try to walk always, with
Christ for my friend.

M. L. Duncan.

WE ARE SEVEN.

————a simple child,
　That lightly draws its breath,
And feels its life in every limb,
　What should it know of death?

I met a little cottage girl:
　She was eight years old, she
　　said;
Her hair was thick with many a
　curl,
　That clustered round her
　　head.

She had a rustic, woodland air,
　And she was wildly clad;
Her eyes were fair, and very fair;
　Her beauty made me glad.

"Sisters and brothers, little maid,
  How many may you be?"
"How many? seven in all," she
    said,
  And wondering looked at me.

"And where are they? I pray
    you tell;"
  She answered, "Seven are we,
And two of us at Conway dwell,
  And two are gone to sea.

"Two of us in the churchyard
    lie,
  My sister and my brother;
And in the churchyard cottage, I
  Dwell near them with my
    mother."

"You say that two at Conway
    dwell,

And two are gone to sea,
Yet ye are seven. I pray you
    tell,
    Sweet maid, how this may be."

Then did the little maid reply,
    "Seven boys and girls are we,
Two of us in the churchyard lie,
    Beneath the churchyard tree."

"You run about, my little maid,
    Your limbs they are alive;
If two are in the churchyard
    laid,
    Then ye are only five."

"Their graves are green, they
    may be seen,"
The little maid replied;

" Twelve steps or more from my
    mother's door,
  And they are side by side.

" My stockings there I often
    knit,
  My kerchief there I hem;
And there upon the ground I
    sit —
  I sit and sing to them

"And often after sunset, sir,
  When it is light and fair,
I take my little porringer,
  And eat my supper there.

" The first that died was sister
    Jane ;
  In bed she moaning lay,

Till God released her from her
    pain,
  An d then she went away.

" So in the churchyard she was
    laid ;
  And, when the grass was dry,
Together round her grave we
    played,
  My brother John and I.

"And when the ground was
    white with snow,
  And I could run and slide,
My brother John was forced to
    go,
  And he lies by her side."

" How many are you then," said
    I,
  " If they two are in heaven?"

Quick was the little maid's reply,
  "O, master! we are seven."

" But they are dead ; those two
    are dead;
  Their spirits are in heaven."
'T was throwing words away;
    for still
The little maid would have her
    will,
  And said, "Nay, we are
    seven."
                      Wordsworth.

ROBERT OF LINCOLN.

Merrily swinging on briar and
    weed,
  Near to the nest of his little
    dame,
Over the mountain side or mead,
  Robert of · Lincoln is telling
    his name.
    Bob-o'link, bob-o'link,
    Spink, spank, spink,
Snug and safe is that nest of
    ours,
Hidden   among   the   summer
    flowers,
    Chee, chee, chee.

Robert of Lincoln is gaily drest,
  Wearing a bright black wed-
    ding coat;

White are his shoulders, and
    white his crest;
  Hear him call, in his merry
    note,
    Bob-o'link, bob-o'link,
    Spink, spank, spink,
Look what a nice new coat is
    mine;
Sure there was never a bird so
    fine,
    Chee, chee, chee.

Robert of Lincoln's Quaker wife,
    Pretty and quiet with plain,
    brown wings,
Passing at home a patient life,
    Broods in the grass while her
    husband sings,
    Bob-o'link, bob-o'link,
Brood, kind creature, you need
    not fear

Theives and robbers while I am
    here,
    Chee, chee, chee.

Modest and shy as a nun is she ;
    One weak chirp is her only
    note.
Braggart, and prince of brag-
    garts, is he,
    Pouring boasts from his little
    throat.
Never was I afraid of man ;
Catch me, cowardly knaves, if
    you can.

Six white eggs on a bed of hay,
    Freckled with purple, a pretty
    sight ;
There, as the mother sits all day,

Robert is singing with all his
  might,
Nice good wife, that never goes
  out,
Keeping house while I frolic
  about.

Soon as the little ones chip the
    shell,
  Six wide mouths are open for
    food ;
Robert of Lincoln bestirs him
    well,
  Gathering seeds for the hun-
    gry brood.
This new life is likely to be
Hard for a young fellow like me.

Robert of Lincoln at length is
    made

Sober with work, and silent
  with care ;
Oft in his holiday garment laid
  Half forgotten that merry air.
Nobody knows but my mate and I
Where our nest and our nest-
  lings lie.

Summer wanes, the children are
  grown ;
  Fun and frolic no more he
  knows,
Robert of Lincoln 's a humdrum
  crone ;
  Off he flies, and we sing as he
  goes,
When you can pipe that merry
  old strain,
Robert of Lincoln, come back
  again.

             W. C. Bryant.

THE CHILD'S WISH IN JUNE.

Mother, mother, the winds are
    at play,
Prithee let me be idle to-day.
Look, dear mother, the flowers
    all lie
Languidly under the bright blue
    sky.
See how slowly the streamlet
    glides ;
Look, how the violet roguishly
    hides ;
Even the butterfly rests on the
    rose;
And scarcely sips the sweets as
    he goes.
Poor Tray is asleep in the noon-
    day sun.

And the flies go about him, one
　　by one;
And pussy sits near, with a
　　sleepy grace,
Without ever thinking of wash-
　　ing her face.
There flies a bird to a neighbor-
　　ing tree ;
But very lazily flieth he,
And he sits and twitters a gen-
　　tle note,
That scarcely ruffles his little
　　throat.

You bid me be busy ; but, moth-
　　er, hear　　　　·
How the humdrum grasshopper
　　soundeth near,
And the soft west wind is so
　　light in its play,

It scarcely moves a leaf on the
    spray.

I wish, oh! I wish I was yonder
    cloud,
That sails about with its misty
    shroud;
Books and work I no more
    should see,
And I'd come and float, dear
    mother, o'er thee.
                Mrs. Gilman.

SONG OF THE SNOW-BIRD.

The ground was all covered with
    snow one day,
And two little sisters were busy
    at play,
When a snow-bird was sitting
    close by on a tree,
And merrily singing his chick-a-
    dee-dee.

He had not been singing that
    tune very long,
Ere Emily heard him, so loud
    was his song ;
" O, sister, look out of the win-
    dow," said she,
" Here 's a dear little bird sing-
    ing chick-a-dee-dee.

"Poor fellow, he walks in the
    snow and the sleet,
And has neither stockings nor
    shoes on his feet;
I pity him so, how cold he must
    be !
And yet he keeps singing his
    chick-a-dee-dee.

"If I were a bare-footed snow-
    bird, I know
I would not stay out in the cold
    and the snow;
I wonder what makes him so
    full of his glee?
He's all the time singing that
    chick-a-dee-dee.

"Oh, mother! do get him some
    stockings and shoes,

And a nice little frock, and a
    hat, if he choose;
I wish he 'd come into the par-
    lor and see
How warm we would make him,
    poor chick-a-dee-dee."

The bird had flown down for
    some pieces of bread,
And heard every word little Em-
    ily said;
"What a figure I 'd make in
    that dress," thought he,
And he laughed as he warbled
    his chick-a-dee-dee.

"I 'm grateful," he said, "for
    'the wish you express,
But I have no occasion for such
    a fine dress;

I had rather remain with my
    limbs all free,
Than be hobbled about, singing
    chick-a-dee-dee.

"There is One, my dear child,
    though I can not tell who,
Has clothed me already, and
    warm enough, too ;
Good morning, oh, who are so
    happy as we ! "
And away he went, singing his
    chick-a-dee-dee.

               Woodworth

THE MAGPIE'S NEST.

A FABLE.

When the arts in their infancy
    were,
    In a fable of old 't is ex
    pressed,
A wise magpie constructed that
    rare
    Little house for young birds,
    called a nest.

This was talked of the whole
    country round,
    You might hear it on every
    bough sung,
" Now, no longer upon the
    rough ground

Will fond mothers brood over
their young ;

" For the magpie, with exqui-
site skill,'
Has invented a moss-covered
cell,
Within which a whole family
will
In the utmost security dwell."

To her mate did each female
bird say,
" Let us fly to the magpie, my
dear ;
If she will but teach us the way,
A nest we will build us up
here.

" It's a thing that's close-arch-
ed over head,

With a hole made to creep
   out and in ;
We, my bird, might make just
   such a bed,
   If we only knew how to be-
   gin."

To the magpie soon every bird
   went,
   And in modest terms made
   their request,
That she would be pleased to
   consent
   To teach them to build up a
   nest

She replied, "I will show you
   the way;
   So observe everything that I
   do:

First, two sticks cross each oth-
    er I lay——"
  "To be sure," said the crow;
  "why, I knew

"It must be begun with two
    sticks,
  And I thought that they
    crossed should be."
Said the pie, "Then some straw
    and moss mix,
  In the way you now see done
    by me."

"Oh, yes, certainly," said the
    jackdaw,
  "That must follow, of course,
    I have thought;
Though I never before building
    saw,

I guessed that without being
    taught."

"More moss, straw, and feathers
    I place,
  In this manner," continued
    the pie.
" Yes, no doubt, madam, that is
    the case ;
  Though no builder myself, so
    thought I."

Whatever she taught them, be-
    side,
  In his turn, every bird of
    them said,
Though the nest-making art he'd
    ne'er tried,
  He had just such a thought in
    his head.

Still, the pie went on showing
    her art,
    Till a nest she had built up
    half-way;
She no more of her skill would
    impart,
    But in anger went fluttering
    away.

And this speech in their hearing
    she made,
    As she perched o'er their
    heads on a tree:
"If ye all were well skilled in my
    trade,
    Pray, why came ye to learn
    it of me?

"When a scholar is willing to
    learn,

He, with silent submission,
  should hear;
Too late they their folly dis-
  cern—
The effect to this day does
  appear;

"For, whenever a pie's nest you
  see,
Her charming warm canopy
  view;   .
All birds' nests but her's seem to
  be
A magpie's nest just cut in
  two."

Melodies for Childhood.

MABEL ON MID-SUMMER DAY.

PART I.

"Arise, my maiden, Mabel,"
  The mother said, "Arise;
For the golden sun of mid-sum-
    mer
  Is shining in the skies.

"Arise, my little maiden;
  For thou must speed away,
To wait upon thy grandmother
  This livelong summer day.

"And thou must carry with thee
  This wheaten cake so fine,
This new-made pat of butter,
  This little flask of wine.

.   3

"And tell the dear old body,
   This day I can not come ;
For the good man went out yes-
   ter-morn,
   And he is not come home.

"And more than this, poor Amy
   Upon my knee doth lie ;
I fear me, with this fever pain,
   The little child will die.

"And thou canst help thy grand-
   mother ;
   The table thou canst spread ;
Canst feed the little dog and
   bird,
   And thou canst make her bed.

"And thou canst fetch the water
   From the Lady-well hard by ;

And thou canst gather from the
    wood
The fagots, brown and dry.

"Canst go down to the lone-
    some glen,
To milk the mother-ewe.
This is the work, my Mabel,
    That thou wilt have to do.

" But listen now, my Mabel,
    This is mid-summer day,
When all the fairy people
    From elf-land come away.

"And when thou 'rt in the lone-
    some glen,
Keep by the running burn,

And do not pluck the strawber-
 ry-flower,
 Nor break the lady-fern;

" But think not of the fairy-
 folk,
 Lest mischief should befall;
Think only of poor Amy,
 And how thou lov'st us all.

" Yet keep good heart my Ma-
 bel,
 If thou the fairies see,
And give them kindly answer,
 If they should speak to thee.

"And when into the fir-wood
 Thou goest for fagots brown,
Do not, like idle children,
 Go wandering up and down;

" But fill thy little apron,
  My child, with earnest speed;
And that thou break no living
      bough
Within the wood, take heed.

" For they are spiteful brownies
  Who in the wood abide;
So be thou careful of this thing,
  Lest evil should betide.

" But think not, little Mabel,
  Whilst thou art in the wood.
'Of the dwarfish, wilful brownies,
  But of the Father good.

"And when thou goest to the
      spring
  To fetch the water thence,
Do not disturb the little stream,
  Lest this should give offence.

" For the queen of all the fairies,
   She loves that water bright ;
I 've seen her drinking there,
   myself,
   On many a summer night.

" But she 's a gracious lady,
   And her thou need'st not
   fear :
Only disturb thou not the stream,
   Nor spill the water clear."

"Now all this I will heed, moth-
   er,
   Will no word disobey,
And wait upon the grandmother
   This livelong summer day."

PART II.

Away tripped little Mabel,

With the wheaten cake so
 fine,
With the new-made pat of butter,
 And the little flask of wine.

And long before the sun was
 hot,
 And summer mist had cleared,
Beside the good old grandmoth-
 er,
 The willing child appeared.

And all her mother's message
 She told with right good-will,
How that the father was away,
 And the little child was ill.

And then she swept the hearth
 up clean,
And then the table spread,

And next she fed the dog and
    bird,
    And then she made the bed.

"And go, now," said the grand-
    mother,
    " Ten paces down the dell,
And bring in water for the day,
    Thou knowest the Lady-well."

The first time that good Mabel
    went,
    Nothing at all saw she,
Except a bird, a sky-blue bird,
    That sat upon a tree.

The next time that good Mabel
    went,
    There sat a lady bright
Beside the well, a lady small,
    All clothed in green and white.

A curtsey low made Mabel,
  And then she stooped to fill
Her pitcher at the sparkling
    spring,
  But no drop did she spill.

"Thou art a handy maiden,"
  The fairy lady said;
" Thou hast not spilled a drop,
    nor yet
  The fairy spring troubled.

"And for this thing which thou
    hast done,
  Yet may not understand,
I give to thee a better gift
  Than houses or than land.

" Thou shalt do well whate'er
    thou dost,

As thou hast done this day ;
Shalt have the will and power to
    please,
And shalt be loved alway."

Thus having said, she passed
    from sight,
And naught could Mabel see
But the little bird, the sky-blue
    bird,
Upon the leafy tree.

"And now go," said the grand-
    mother,
"And fetch in fagots dry ;
All in the neighboring fir-wood,
    Beneath the trees they lie."

Away went kind, good Mabel,
    Into the fir-wood near,

Where all the ground was dry
   and brown,
And the grass grew thin and
   sere.

She did not wander up and down,
   Nor yet a live branch pull ;
But steadily of the fallen boughs
   She picked her apron full.

And when the wild-wood brownies,
   Came sliding to her mind,
She drove them thence, as she
   wa told,
   With home thoughts, sweet
   and kind.

But all that while, the brownies,
   Within the fir-wood still,

They watched her how she pick.
    ed the wood,
And strove to do no ill.

"And, oh! but she is small and
    neat,"
  Said one, "'t were shame to
    spite
A creature so demure and weak,
  A creature harmless quite."

"Look only," said another,
  "At her little gown of blue;
At her kerchief pinned about
    her head,
And at her little shoe."

"Oh! but she is a comely
    child,"
  Said a third, "and we will lay

A good-luck penny in her path,
  A boon for her this day,
Seeing she broke no living wood,
  No live thing did affray."

With that, the smallest penny,
  Of the finest silver ore,
Upon the dry and slippery path
  Lay Mabel's feet before.

With joy she picked the penny
    up,
  The fairy penny good;
And with the fagots, dry and
    brown,
  Went wandering from the
    wood.

"Now she has that," said the
    brownies,

"Let flax be ever so dear,
'T will buy her clothes of the
   very best
For many and many a year."

"And go, now," said the grand-
   mother,
"Since falling is the dew,
Go down unto the lonesome glen,
   And milk the mother-ewe."

All down into the lonesome glen,
   Through copses thick and
   wild,
Through moist rank grass, by
   twinkling streams,
Went on the willing child.

And when she came to the lonesome glen,

She kept beside the burn,
And neither plucked the straw-
    berry-flower,
Nor broke the lady-fern.

And while she milked the moth-
    er-ewe,
Within this lonesome glen,
She wished that little Amy
    Were strong and well again.

And soon as she had thought
    this thought,
She heard a coming sound,
As if a thousand fairy-folk
    Were gathering all around.

And then she heard a little
    voice,
Shrill as the midge's wing,

That spake aloud, "A human child
    Is here; yet mark this thing:

"The lady-fern is all unbroke,
    The strawberry-flower un-
    ta'en;
What shall be done for her who still
    From mischief can refrain?"

"Give her a fairy cake," said one;
    "Grant her a wish," said
    three;
"The latest wish that she hath
    wished,"
Said all, "whate'er it be."

Kind Mabel heard the words
    they spoke.

And from the lonesome glen,
Unto the good old grandmother
Went gladly back again.

Thus happened it to Mabel,
  On that mid-summer day,
And these three fairy blessings
  She took with her away.

'T is good to make all duty
    sweet,
  To be alert and kind ;
'T is good, like little Mabel,
  To have a willing mind.
                    Mary Howitt.
            4

CASABIANCA.

The boy stood on the burning
    deck,
  Whence all but him had fled;
The flame that lit the battle's
    wreck,
  Shone round him o'er tho
    dead.

Yet beautiful and bright ho
    stood,
  As born to rule the storm;
A creature of heroic blood,
  A proud though childlike
    form.

The flames rolled on, he would
    not go,
  Without his father's word.

That father, faint in death below,
  His voice no longer heard.

He called aloud, "Say, father,
    say,
  If yet my task be done!"
He knew not that the chieftain
    lay
  Unconscious of his son.

"Speak, father!" once again he
    cried,
  "If I may yet begone!"
And but the booming shots re-
    plied,
  And fast the flames rolled on.

Upon his brow he felt their
    breath,
  And in his waving hair;

And looked, from that lone post
    of death,
  In still, yet brave, despair.

And shouted but once more
    aloud,
  "My father, must I stay ? "
While o'er him fast, through
    sail and shroud,
  The wreathing fires made way.

They wrapped the ship in splen-
    dor wild,
  They caught the flag on high,
And streamed above the gallant
    child,
  Like banners in the sky.

There came a burst of thunder-
    sound !

The boy—oh! where was he!
Ask of the winds that far around
　With fragments strewed the
　sea.

With mast, and helm, and pen-
　non fair,
　That well had borne their
　part—
But the noblest thing which per-
　ished there
　Was that young and faithful
　heart.

Mrs. Hemans.

THE SPIDER AND THE FLY.

" Will you walk into my parlor,"
 said the spider to the fly ;
" 'T is the prettiest little parlor
 that ever you did spy ;
The way into my parlor is up a
 winding stair,
And I have many curious things
 to show when you are there."

" Oh, no, no ! " said the little fly,
 " to ask me is in vain ;
For who goes up your winding
 stain can ne'er come down
 again."
"I 'm sure you must be weary,
 dear, with soaring up so high ;
Will you rest upon my little

bed ? " said the spider to the
fly.

" There   are   pretty   curtains
    drawn around, the sheets are
    fine and thin ;
And if you like to rest awhile,
    I 'll snugly tuck you in."
" Oh, no, no ! " said the little
    fly, " for I've often heard it
    said,
They never, never wake again,
    who sleep upon your bed."

Said the cunning spider to the
    fly, " Dear friend, what can I
    do
To prove the warm affection I
    have always felt for you ?

I have within my pantry good
    store of all that's nice;
I'm sure you're very welcome,
    will you please to take a
    slice?"

"Oh, no, no!" said the little fly,
    "kind sir, that can not be;
I've heard what's in your pan-
    try, and I do not wish to see."
"Sweet creature," said the spi-
    der, " you're witty and you're
    wise ;
How handsome are your gauzy
    wings! how brilliant are your
    eyes!

"I have a little looking-glass
    upon my parlor shelf;
If you'll step in one moment,

dear, you shall behold your-
self."
"I thank you gentle sir," she
    said, "for what you 're pleased
    to say ;
And bidding you good morning,
    now, I 'll call another day."

The spider turned him round
    about, and went into his den ;
For well he knew the silly fly
    would soon come back again :
So he wove a subtle web, in a
    little corner sly,
And he set his table ready, to
    dine upon the fly.

Then he came out to his door
    again, and merrily did sing,

" Come hither, hither, pretty fly,
  with the pearl and silver wing.
Your robes are green and purple, there's a crest upon your
  head ;
Your eyes are like the diamond
  bright, but mine are dull as
  lead ! "

Alas, alas ! how very soon this
  silly little fly,
Hearing his wily flattering words,
  came slowly flitting by ;
With buzzing wings she hung
  aloft, then near and nearer
  drew,
Thinking only of her brilliant
  eyes, and green and purple
  hue.

Thinking only of her crested
  head, poor foolish thing, at
  last,
Up jumped the cunning spider,
  and fiercely held her fast;
He dragged her up his winding
  stair, into his dismal den,
Within his little parlor, but she
  ne'er came out again.

And now, dear little children,
  who may this story read,
To idle, silly, flattering words, I
  pray you, ne'er give heed.
Unto an evil counsellor, close
  heart, and ear, and eye,
And take a lesson from this tale
  of the spider and the fly.
Mary Howitt.

THE BLIND BOY AT PLAY.

The blind boy's been at play,
 mother,
  The merry games we had;
We led him on his way, mother,
  And every step was glad;
But when we found a starry
  flower,
  And praised its varied hue,
A tear came trembling down his
  cheek,
  Just like a drop of dew.

We took him to the mill, moth-
  er,
  Where falling waters made
A rainbow o'er the hills, mother,

As golden sun-rays played;
But when we shouted at the
    scene,
    And hailed the clear blue sky,
He stood quite still upon the
    bank,
    And breathed a long, long
    sigh.

We asked him why he wept,
    mother,
    Whene'er we found the spots
Where periwinkles crept, moth-
    er,
    O'er wild forget-me-nots.
"Ah me," he said, while tears
    ran down
    As fast as summer showers,
" It is because I can not see
    The sunshine and the flow-
    ers."

Oh! that poor sightless boy,
    mother,
  He taught me that I 'm blest;
For I can look with joy, mother,
  On all I love the best;
And when I see the dancing
    stream,
  And daises red and white,
I kneel upon the meadow-sod,
  And thank my God for sight.

                    Eliza Cook.

CHRISTMAS TIMES.

'Twas the night before Christmas, and all through the house
Not a creature was stirring, not
   even a mouse.
The stockings were hung by the
   chimney, with care,
In the hope that St. Nicholas
   soon would be there.
The children were nestled all
   snug in their beds,
While visions of sugar-plums
   danced in their heads ;
And mamma in her kerchief,
   and I in my cap,
Had just settled ourselves for a
   long winter's nap ;
When, out on the lawn, there
   arose such a clatter,

I sprang from the bed to see
what was the matter.
Away to the window I flew like
a flash,
Tore open the window, and
threw up the sash.
The moon on the breast of the
new-fallen snow,
Gave the luster of mid-day to
objects below ;
When what to my wondering
eyes should appear,
But a miniature sleigh, and eight
tiny reindeer,
With a little, old driver so live-
ly and quick :
I knew in a moment it must be
St. Nick.
More rapid than eagles his cour-
sers they came.

And he whistled, and shouted,
and called them by name:
"Now, Dasher! now, Dancer!
now, Prancer! now, Vixen!
On, Comet! on, Cupid! on, Dun-
der and Blixen!
To the top of the porch, to the
top of the wall,
Now dash away, dash away,
dash away, all!"
As dry leaves, that before the
wild hurricane fly,
When they meet with an obsta-
cle, mount to the sky,
So up to the house-top the cour-
sers they flew,
With the sleigh full of toys, and
St. Nicholas, too;
And then, in a twinkling, I heard
on the roof,

5

The prancing and pawing of
  each little hoof;
As I drew in my head, and was
  turning around,
Down the chimney St. Nicholas
  came, with a bound.
He was dressed all in fur, from
  his head to his foot,
And his clothes were all tarnish-
  ed with ashes and soot;
A bundle of toys he had flung
  on his back,
And he looked like a pedlar just
  opening his pack.
His eyes, how they twinkled!
  his dimples, how merry!
His cheeks were like roses, his
  nose like a cherry.
His droll little mouth was drawn
  up, like a bow,

And the beard of his chin was
    as white as the snow;
The stump of a pipe he held
    tight in his teeth,
And the smoke it encircled his
    head like a wreath.
He was chubby and plump, a
    right jolly old elf,
And I laughed when I saw him,
    in spite of myself.
A wink of his eye, and a twist of
    his head,
Soon gave me to know I had
    nothing to dread.
He spoke not a word, but went
    straight to his work,
And filled all his stockings; then
    turned, with a jerk,
And laying his finger aside of
    his nose,

And giving a nod, up the chimney he rose.
He sprang to his sleigh, to his
team gave a whistle,
And away they all flew, like the
down of a thistle;
But I heard him exclaim, ere he
drove out of sight,
"Merry Christmas to all, and to
all a good night!"

O. C. Moore.

PUSSY CAT.

Pussy cat lives in the servants'
    hall,
    She can set up her back, and
        purr.
The little mice live in a crack in
    the wall,
    But they hardly dare venture
        to stir.

For, whenever they think of ta-
    king the air,
    Or filling their little maws,
The pussy cat says, " Come out,
    if you dare;
    I will catch you all with my
    claws."

Scrabble, scrabble, scrabble,
  went all the little mice,
    For they smelt the Cheshire
    cheese;
The pussy cat said, "It smells
  very nice;
    Now, do come out, if you
    please."

"Squeak," said the little mouse,
    "Squeak, squeak, squeak,"
Said all the young ones, too;
"We never creep out when cats
  are about;
    Because we are afraid of you."

So the cunning old cat lay down
  on a mat.
    By the fire in the servants'
    hall;
"If the little mice peep, they'll
  think I'm asleep;"

So she rolled herself up like a
ball.

"Squeak," said the little mouse,
   " we 'll creep out,
And eat some Cheshire cheese;
That silly old cat is asleep on the
   mat,
   And we may sup at our ease."

Nibble, nibble, nibble, went the
   little mice,
   And they licked their little
   paws;
Then the cunning old cat sprang
   up from the mat,
And caught them all with her
   claws.
Aunt Effie —Melodies for Child-
                  [hood.

WHO STOLE THE BIRD'S NEST?

To whit, to whit, to whee!
Will you listen to me?
Who stole four eggs I laid,
And the nice nest I made?

" Not I," said the cow," Moo-oo!
Such a thing I 'd never do;
I gave you a wisp of hay,
But did n't take your nest away.
Not I," said the cow, " Moo-oo!
Such a thing I 'd never do."

To whit, to whit, to whee!
Will you listen to me?
Who stole four eggs I laid,
And the nice nest I made?

" Bob-o'-link, bob-o'-link !
Now, what do you think !
Who stole a nest away
From the plum-tree, to-day ? "

"Not I," said the dog, " Bow,
    wow !
I would n't be so mean, I vow;
I gave hairs the nest to make,
But the nest I did not take.
Not I," said the dog, " Bow,
    wow !
I would n't be so mean, I vow."

To whit, to whit, to whee !
Will you listen to me ?
Who stole four eggs I laid,
And the nice nest I made?

Bob-o'-link, bob-o'-link !

Now, what do you think!
Who stole a nest away
From the plum-tree, to day ?"

"Coo-coo, coo-coo, coo-coo!
Let me speak a word, too.
Who stole that pretty nest
From little yellow breast ?

"Not I," said the sheep, "Oh,
        no!
I would n't treat a poor bird so.
I gave the wool the nest to line,
But the nest was none of mine.
Baa, baa!" said the sheep, "oh,
        no!
I would n't treat a poor bird so."

To whit, to whit, to whee!
Will you listen to me ?

Who stole four eggs I laid,
And the nice nest I made

" Bob-o'-link, bob-o'-link !
Now, what do you think !
Who stole a nest away
From the plum-tree, to-day ? "

" Coo-coo, coo-coo, coo-coo !
Let me speak a word too.
Who stole that pretty nest
From little yellow breast ?"

" Caw, caw ! " cried the crow,
" I should like to know
What thief took away
A bird's nest to-day."

" Cluck, cluck ! " said the hen,
" Do n't ask me again.
Why, I hav'n't a chick

Would do such a trick.
We all gave her a feather,
And she wove them together.
I'd scorn to intrude
On her and her brood.
Cluck, cluck!" said the hen,
" Do n't ask me again."

" Chirr-a-whirr, chirr-a-whirr!
We will make a great stir!
Let us find out his name,
And all cry, for shame!"

" I would not rob a bird,"
    Said little Mary Green;
" I think, I never heard
    Of anything so mean."
" 'T is very cruel, too,"
    Said little Alice Neal;

" I wonder if he knew
    How sad the bird would feel."

A little boy hung down his head,
And went and hid behind the
        bed ;
For *he* stole that pretty nest
From poor little yellow breast;
And he felt so full of shame,
He did n't like to tell his name,
        Melodies for Childhood.

THE MATCH GIRL.

BY HANS CHRISTIAN ANDERSON.

Little Gretchen, little Gretchen,
  Wanders up and down the
    street;
The snow is on her yellow hair,
  The frost is at her feet.

The rows of long dark houses,
  Without, look cold and damp,
By the struggling of the moon-
    beam,
  By the flicker of the lamp.

The clouds ride fast as horses,
  The wind is from the north,
But no one cares for Gretchen,
  And no one looketh forth.

Within those dark, damp hous-
    es,
  Are merry faces bright,
And happy hearts are watching
    out
  The old year's latest night.

The board is spread with plenty,
  Where the smiling kindred
    meet;
But the frost is on the pavement,
  And the beggar's in the
    street.

With the little box of matches
  She could not sell all day,
And the thin, thin tattered man-
    tle
  The wind blows every way

She clingeth to the railing,
    She shivers in the gloom ;
There are parents, sitting snugly
    By firelight in the room ;

And groups of busy children,
    Withdrawing just the tips
Of rosy fingers pressed in vain
    Against their bursting lips,

With grave and earnest faces,
    Are whispering to each other,
Of presents for the new year,
        made
For father, or for mother.

But no one talks to Gretchen,
    And no one hears her speak ;
No breath of little whispers
    Comes warmly to her cheek.

No little arms are round her;
  Ah me! that there should be,
With so much happiness on
    earth,
  So much of misery!

Sure, they of many blessings
  Should scatter blessings round,
As laden boughs in autumn
    fling
  Their ripe fruits to the ground.

And the best love man can offer
  To the God of love, be sure,
Is kindness to His little ones,
  And bounty to His poor.

Little Gretchen, little Gretchen,
  Goes coldly on her way;

6

There's no one looketh out at
    her,
  There's no one bids her stay.

. Her home is cold and desolate,
    No smile, no food, no fire ;
But   children   clamorous for
    bread,
  And an impatient sire.

So she sits down in an angle,
    Where two great houses meet,
And she curleth up beneath her,
    For warmth, her little feet.

And she looketh on the cold
    wall,
  And on the colder sky,
And wonders if the little stars
    Are bright fires up on high.

She heard a clock strike slowly,
  Up in a far church tower,
With such a sad and solemn
    tone,
  Telling the midnight hour.

And she thought, as she sat
    lonely,
  And listened to the chime,
Of woudrous things that she had
    loved
  To hear in olden time.

And she remembered her of
    tales
  Her mother used to tell,
And of the cradle songs she
    sang,
  When summer's twilight fell.

Of good men, and of angels,

And of the Holy Child,
Who was cradled in a manger,
  When winter was most wild.

Who was poor, and cold, and
    hungry,
  And desolate, and lone ;
And she thought the song had
    told her,
  He was ever with His own.

And all the poor and hungry,
  And forsaken ones are His ;
"How good of Him to look on
    me,
In such a place as this ! "

Colder it grew and colder,
  But she does not heed it now,
For the pressure at her heart,

And the weight upon her
  brow.

But she struck one little match
  On the wall, so cold and bare,
That she might look around her,
  And see if He was there.

The single match has kindled,
  And, by the light it threw,
It seemed to little Gretchen
  The wall was rent in two.

And she could see the room
  within,
  The room, all warm and
  bright,
With the fire-glow, red and
  dusky,
  And the tapers all alight.

And there were kindred gath-
    ered
  Round the table richly spread,
With heaps of goodly viands,
  Red wine and pleasant bread.

She could smell the pleasant sa-
    vor,
  She could hear what they did
    say;
Then all was darkness once
    again—
  The match was burnt away.

She struck another, hastily,
  And now she seemed to see,
Within the same warm chamber
  A glorious Christmas tree.

The branches were all laden

With such things as children
    prize ;
Bright gifts for boy and maiden,
    She saw them with her eyes.

And she almost seemed to touch
    them,
    And to join the welcome
    shout,
When darkness fell around her ;
    For the little match was out.

Another, yet another, she
    Has tried ; they will not light,
'Till all her little store she took,
    And struck with all her might.

And the whole miserable place
    Was lighted with the glare ;
And lo, there hung a little child
    Before her, in the air.

There were blood-drops on His
   forehead,
   And a spear-wound in His side,
And cruel nail-prints in his feet,
   And in His hands spread wide.

And He looked upon her gently;
   And she felt that He had
   known
Pain, hunger, cold, and sorrow,
   Ay, equal to her own.

And He pointed to the laden
   board,
   And to the Christmas tree,
Then up to the cold sky, and
   said,
   "Will Gretchen come with
   me?"

The poor child felt her pulses
    fail,
  She felt her eyeballs swim ;
And a ringing sound was in her
    ears,
  Like her dead mother's hymn.

And she folded both her thin,
    white hands,
  And turned from that bright
    board,
And from the golden gifts, and
    said,
  "With Thee, with Thee, oh,
    Lord."

The chilly winter morning
  Breaks up in the dull skies,
On the city wrapped in vapor,

On the spot where Gretchen
lies.

In her scant and tattered gar-
ment,
  With her back against the
wall,
She sitteth, cold and rigid;
  She answers not their call.

They have lifted her up fearful-
ly ;
  They shuddered, as they said,
" It was a bitter, bitter night,
  The child is frozen dead."

The angels sang their greeting,
  For one more redeemed from
sin ;
Men said, " It was a bitter night;
  Would no one let her in ?"

And they shuddered as they
   spoke of her,
   And sighed—they could not
   see
How much of happiness there
   was
   With so much misery.

THE CHESNUT PARTY.

Merrily sang the cricket forth,
  One fair October night,
And the stars looked down, and
    the northern crown
  Gave its strange, fantastic light.

A nipping frost was in the air,
  On flowers and grass it fell;
And the leaves were still on the
    eastern hill,
  As if touched by a fairy spell.

To the very top of the tall nut
    trees,
  The frost king seemed to ride;
With his wand he stirs the ches-
    nut burrs,
  And straight they are opened
    wide.

And squirrels and children to-
gether dream
Of the coming winter's hoard;
And many, I ween, are the ches-
nuts seen
In hole or in garret stored.

The children are sleeping in
feather beds,
Poor Bun in his mossy nest.
He courts repose, with his tail
on his nose,
On the others warm blankets
rest.

Late in the morning the sun gets
up
From behind the village spire,
And the childr.. dream that the
first ·u gleam
Is the chesnut tr es on fire.

The squirrel had on, when he
    first awoke,
      All the clothing he could com-
      mand;
And his breakfast was light, he
    just took a bite
      Of an acorn that lay at hand.

And then he was off to the trees
    to work,
      While the children some time
      it takes
To dress and to eat what they
    think meet
      Of coffee and buckwheat cakes.

"Oh, there is a heap of ches-
    nuts, see!"
      Cried the youngest of the train,
For they came to a stone where
    the squirrel had thrown
      What he meant to pick up again.

And two bright eyes from the
    tree o'erhead
Looked down on the open bag
Where the nuts went in, and so
    to begin,
    Almost made his courage flag.

Away on the hill, outside the
    wood,
    Three giant trees there stand,
And the chesnuts bright that
    hang in sight
    Are eyed by the youthful band.

And one of their number climbs
    a tree,
    And passes from bough to
    bough ;
And the children run, for, with
    pelting fun,
    The nuts fall thickly now.

    *   *   *   *

To run beneath the shaking tree,
  And then to scamper away,
And with laughing shout to
    dance about
  The grass where the chesnuts
    lay.

With flowing dresses and blow-
    ing hair,
  And eyes that no shadow
    knew,
  Like the growing light of a
    morning bright,
  The dawn of the summer blue.

The work was ended, the trees
    were stripped,
  The children were " tired of
    play ; "
And they forgot, but the squirrel
    did not,
  The wrong they had done that
    day.   Miss Warner.